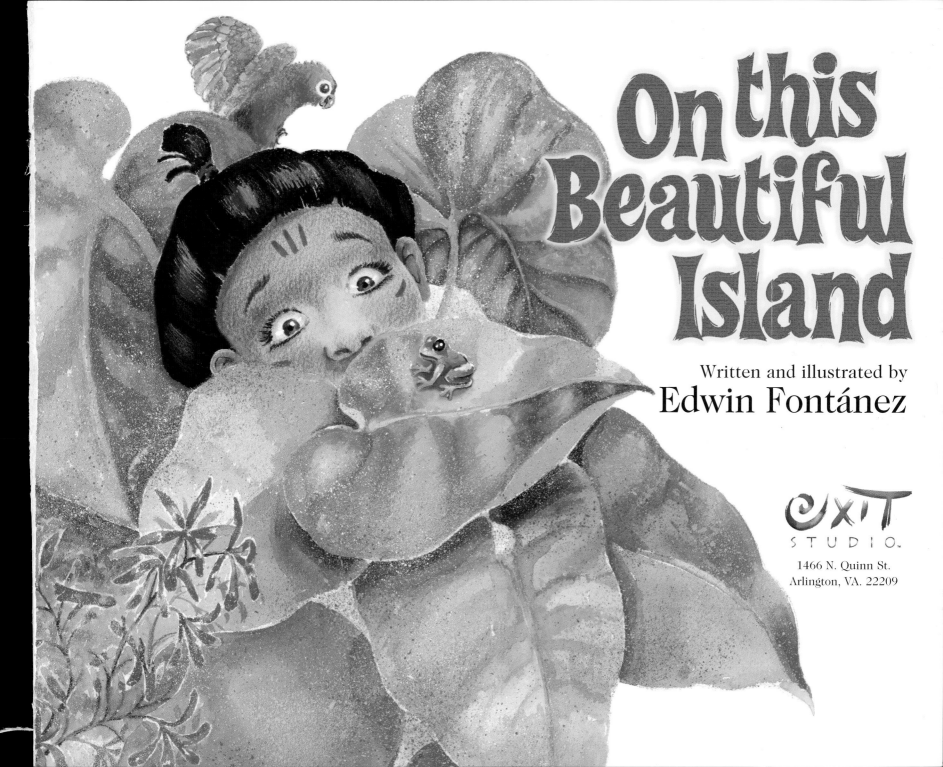

On this Beautiful Island

Written and illustrated by
Edwin Fontánez

EXIT
STUDIO.

1466 N. Quinn St.
Arlington, VA. 22209

On this beautiful island,

as far as my eyes can see,

the early sun runs shiny fingers

through bright green and golden leaves.

Deep in the heart of this beautiful land,

blue skies, green mountains,

and the ocean embrace as one.

The wind plays and pushes lazy clouds

and makes the tall palm trees

giggle and dance.

Guanín is the name mother and father call me.

I am the guardian of this forest.

I am the keeper of the river,

the sea, and all breathing trees.

This is Tahite my little green parrot.

She is my close-to-the-heart friend.

She loves to chirp loudly in my ear

and gossip with other birds.

We share a love for the ocean, the sun,

and ripe yellow guavas!

Welcome to our home.

I'm so glad you could come.

Let me take you to where

the tiny hummingbird nestles

and shy flowers doze off

under the warm shade

of the big Ceiba tree.

Come along now, don't stay behind!

There is so much I want you to see.

Look around and pay close attention.

Learn the song of the river and the ocean

that floats on the wind.

Before we go on our adventure

there is something you should know:

Remember the words of wisdom

that father and mother taught me.

Be careful where we step

and be careful what we do,

for the forest is full of life like you and me.

Let's fill up our eyes with nature's colors

and always be gentle

to the creatures around us.

So get ready. Here we go!

Let Tahite and me take you to places

you've never seen before...

Oh, what a beautiful day in my village! Oh, what a beautiful land! Come and help us gather the crops!

Let's have some fun with my friends in the field...

This is my secret place by the river,

where we can sit in the shade.

Would you like to taste a ripe yellow guava?

Do you want to hear the river sing?

Where am I going? Where am I going?

the mountain river calls out happily rolling downstream.

Blurb, blurb, I'm running in circles.

It speaks to me! The river speaks to me!

I have to go now. I can't stop to chat...

The river tells me stories in its own special way.

Jumping over pebbles that sparkle like crystals,

with beautiful sounds louder than words.

Now it's time to go deep into the forest!

Prepare yourself for a special treat...

ko-kee

Listen to the song that moves mountains

from a frog as small as your thumb!

Meet the Coquí...See how tiny he is?

Listen closely to the sound of his song!

Ko-kee, Ko-kee is the song in my dreams.

Ko-kee, Ko-kee is my favorite sound.

Coquí, Coquí sits on top of a leaf.

Beautiful rainy days are his favorite kind.

ko-kee ko-kee ko-kee ko-kee

Squint your eyes and look up to the clouds

hanging in the bright blue sky.

Close your eyes and turn your face up,

and feel the breeze touching your skin.

Here in the forest, the birds and the wind

hide among the leaves that hang from the trees.

Did you see a fast hummingbird

hovering close to a red flower?

In the blink of an eye he rushes away,

his tiny head dusted with pollen.

Look far away into the distance.

Can you see what I see?

Can you hear the crashing of waves?

Can you hear the song of the seagulls?

Are you ready to guess

where we'll be going next?

Hurry! Come along with me to the shore.

Let's follow the high sun down to the bay.

Listen to the roar of the blue ocean.

The sun makes the waves sparkle

like silver fireflies!

Ahg-Whaaash! Soak your feet!

Ahg-Whaaash! Soak your feet!

Sing out the foamy salt waves...

Ahg-Whaaash! Soak your toes!

Ahg-Whaaash! Soak your toes!

Sings out the ocean again.

Let's take a seat in this shady spot.

Come on and slip off your shoes.

Kick off the sand and watch

the fishermen spread out their nets

then listen to the ocean

inside my pink shell...

Ever since I was a small boy

I've always wondered aloud,

"Father, how long have I loved the sea?"

And he would lift me up,

high up on his shoulders and

laughing loudly answer,

"Ever since you were no bigger

than a conch shell..."

Now the sun goes to sleep and the night spreads over the village...

Crickety-crick cry out happy crickets.

Coquí, Coquí...sings his sweet song out loud.

Close your eyes.

Can you hear the evening music?

Even the night in my village has its own song.

Watch the sky hide under its favorite blanket made of soft rain and fat clouds.

A shiny moon rises up from the shadows, and silver stars blink their diamond eyes.

The night winds cool down the valley.

A crackling bonfire brightens up our home and

long, dark shadows dance their way up the walls.

Everything slows down.

The night is soft, warm, and calm...

It is time to gather in prayer.

It is time to sit around the warm fire,

mother and father, Tahite and me.

It is time to say goodbye to the light of day,

to the rain over blue mountains,

to say good night to Mother Earth.

We pray for the good spirits that live in the forest

and the animals laying themselves to sleep.

I say good night to mother and father,

the river, and the blue sky, too.

I love my land, the coquí, and my home,

and the bright light dancing around the moon.

It is time to say good night to you, too.

Did you enjoy our day in the sun?

Don't forget what you've learned today.

Think of Tahite and me. We're your new friends.

Think of me by blue mountains.

Think of me by the running stream.

Always remember the song of the ocean,

the forest, and the river too...

Also remember the flight of the seagulls

and the soft colors of shells.

Think of the bonfire that warms up my home

and fishermen spreading their nets.

On this beautiful island

as far as your eyes can see,

I hope you know now

that my ocean is also your sea!

A time will come when you'll understand

our paths may never be the same,

but when you wish to be here with us again,

just close your eyes and remember my name...

Here a *cacique* (village chief) is having his body decorated with *pintaderas* before performing a religious ceremony. A *pintadera* is a clay seal which imprints a tattoo. These painted tattoos had various purposes. Sometimes they were used as ceremonial symbols, but also the red pigment extracted from the red *achiote* (annato) seed served as a protection against mosquito bites.

ABOUT THE TAÍNOS

The Taíno (tie-EE-noh) culture dates back more than 2,000 years. Their name comes from the Arawak language and means "good" or "noble." Arawak was also the name for the natives that lived before the 17th century throughout the Greater Antilles (Cuba, Jamaica, Puerto Rico, Dominican Republic, and the Bahamas), so the Taínos are a "family" of the Arawaks. The farmers and fishermen of this island were the original inhabitants of Puerto Rico, known then as *Borikén* (boh-ree-KEN). Even today, you might hear some people call Puerto Rico "Borinquen" and Puerto Ricans "boricuas." The Taíno culture had an intimate connection to nature and a respect for the cycle of life. Their sense of family and cooperation created a strong community.

The Taínos left behind traces of a rich, creative society. Many sites have been uncovered in the Caribbean filled with petroglyphs (rock drawings), ball fields, and the tools and implements of their daily lives. Their influence can still be felt today in words such as *barbecue*, *tobacco*, *canoe*, and *hammock* that are derived from the Arawak language.

You can find out more about the Taínos in Exit Studio's video *Taíno: Guanín's Story* and its companion activity book or visit the website exitstudio.com for additional information and activities.

RIDDLE:
On this beautiful island,
while you were with Tahíte and me,
during our walk in the forest,
how many Coquíes did you see?

Answer at the bottom of the page.

DEDICATION

For Stephanie, Wylie, Mavis, and Scott: the newest Taínos.
For Titi Juana and my parents Doña Ana y Don Modesto.

ACKNOWLEDGMENTS

My most heartfelt gratitude and thanks to Scott Bushnell,
Pam Bushnell, Deborah Menkart, and Barbara Ault. To my
dear new friend Naomi Ayala who made the story come
together. Also to my many friends who always offered their
faith and kind words of encouragement.

–E.F.

Published by:
Exit Studio
1466 North Quinn Street, Arlington, VA 22209
www.exitstudio.com

ISBN: 0-9640868-6-7

Library of Congress Control Number: 2003093972

Printed in Hong Kong

First Edition, 2004
Book Design by Edwin Fontánez
Art Direction and Title Design by Scott Bushnell

Edwin Fontánez's original illustrations were done in opaque gouache and colored pencil
on paper. Guanín and Tahite are original characters copyrighted by Edwin Fontánez and
Exit Studio.

Answer to riddle: 13 Coquíes